BILL AND BEN

Based on *The Railway Series* by the Rev. W. Awdry

Illustrations by
Robin Davies

EGMONT

First published in Great Britain 2004
by Egmont Books Limited
239 Kensington High Street, London W8 6SA
All Rights Reserved

Thomas the Tank Engine & Friends

A BRITT ALLCROFT COMPANY PRODUCTION

Based on The Railway Series by The Rev W Awdry

© Gullane (Thomas) LLC 2004

ISBN 1 4052 1036 2
7 9 10 8
Printed in Great Britain

This is a story about Bill and Ben the twin engines. They worked at the Quarry and they found it very boring. Then one day, something happened that made them realise the Quarry was quite exciting after all!

Bill and Ben worked at the Quarry. The twin engines loved excitement and they often found the Quarry boring. One morning, they were busy moving trucks.

"Listen Bill," said Ben. "Can you hear something?"

"What sort of something?" asked Bill.

"Something different," replied Ben.

"I can't hear anything different," said Bill.

"Exactly," huffed Ben. "Everything is the same – sounds the same, looks the same."

"What we need is a surprise," said Bill.

"What sort of surprise?" asked Ben. But before Bill could answer, the Quarry Master arrived.

"I have just received a message from The Fat Controller," he said. "He wants you to go and see him at the Harbour."

"I wonder what we've done wrong this time," said Bill to Ben, anxiously.

At the Harbour, The Fat Controller was waiting for them.

"Edward is taking the children on a special trip today," he said. "So I want you to go to the Harbour station and look after his trucks."

"We'll do our best, Sir," said the twins. And they *wheeshed* away, relieved that they hadn't done anything wrong after all.

When Bill and Ben arrived at the station, Gordon spoke to them severely. "You must behave here," he said. "You're on the main line now – not at the Quarry."

"Actually, Gordon," giggled Ben, "when we saw you, we thought we were in the scrap yard!"

Gordon was so cross he couldn't think what to say. "Just make sure that my coaches are ready for my evening train," he spluttered as he fumed away.

The twins set to work.

"This will be easy," they said to each other. "We know all about trucks."

But they weren't used to the Harbour trucks, and the trucks knew it.

"We'll show you around," the trucks said to Bill and Ben. "We want to help."

Bill and Ben should have known better than to believe them.

The trucks told Bill and Ben to put things in all the wrong places. Soon the Yard was in a dreadful muddle.

When Gordon saw what had happened, he was furious.

"You've blocked me in," he said to Bill and Ben. "Now my evening train will be late!"

The Troublesome Trucks giggled and giggled.

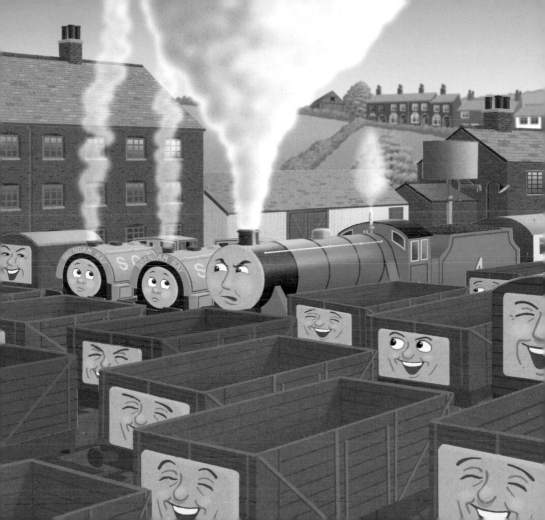

When The Fat Controller found out what had happened, he spoke severely to Bill and Ben.

"I thought I could trust you to work with trucks," he said. "But I was wrong. Now go and sort out this mess!"

Gordon waited impatiently while Bill and Ben put everything back in its proper place. By the time Gordon was able to leave, it was very late indeed. His passengers were furious.

Bill and Ben were sent back to the Quarry in disgrace. As they began work the next day, Ben sighed loudly.

"Back at the boring old Quarry," he said. "And still no sign of a surprise."

Just then, there was a loud rumbling.

"That's a strange noise," gasped Bill. "I've never heard a noise like that before."

"*I* have," whispered his Driver nervously. "It sounds like a rock slide to me."

Then the alarm came.

"DANGER! CLEAR THE QUARRY!" shouted the Quarry Master.

Workmen scrambled into Bill and Ben's trucks, and the twins pulled them away. Rocks were just beginning to tumble down into the Quarry.

"Thank goodness we're here," said the twins. "Otherwise all these people could have been hurt!"

They were just puffing out of the Quarry when they heard a cry –

A workman had been left behind!

"Help! Wait for me!" he cried.

Ben waited as the man scrambled over the fallen rocks to reach the train. He climbed aboard, and the twins pulled out of the Quarry ...

… just in time!

With a huge CRRRASH hundreds of rocks poured down the sides of the Quarry. Everyone was safely out of the way, but there was rubble everywhere.

At that moment, Edward arrived with The Fat Controller.

"Oh dear," said Bill. "This wasn't our fault. I hope The Fat Controller won't be cross with us again."

But he wasn't.

"Bill and Ben," The Fat Controller said. "You may have a lot to learn about trucks, but you behaved quickly and bravely in an emergency. So, three cheers for Bill and Ben, our heroes."

"Hip, hip, hooray!" cried Edward and all the workmen.

"Oh, thank you, Sir," said Bill. "Being called heroes, well it's ... it's ..."

"It's a really nice surprise!" laughed Ben.

The Thomas Story Library is THE definitive collection of stories about Thomas and ALL his Friends.

5 more Thomas Story Library titles will be chuffing into your local bookshop in Summer 2006:

Fergus
Mighty Mac
Harvey
Rusty
Molly

And there are even more
Thomas Story Library books to follow later!
So go on, start your Thomas Story Library NOW!

A Fantastic Offer for Thomas the Tank Engine Fans!

In every Thomas Story Library book like this one, you will find a special token. Collect 6 Thomas tokens and we will send you a brilliant Thomas poster, and a double-sided bedroom door hanger!
Simply tape a £1 coin in the space above, and fill out the form overleaf.

TO BE COMPLETED BY AN ADULT

To apply for this great offer, ask an adult to complete the coupon below and send it with a pound coin and 6 tokens, to:
THOMAS OFFERS, PO BOX 715, HORSHAM RH12 5WG

☐ Please send a Thomas poster and door hanger. I enclose 6 tokens plus a £1 coin. (Price includes P&P)

Fan's name..

Address..

....Postcode....................................

Date of birth...

Name of parent/guardian...

Signature of parent/guardian...

Please allow 28 days for delivery. Offer is only available while stocks last. We reserve the right to change the terms of this offer at any time and we offer a 14 day money back guarantee. This does not affect your statutory rights.

☐ Data Protection Act: If you do not wish to receive other similar offers from us or companies we recommend, please tick this box. Offers apply to UK only.